Ted's Party Bus

by Hilary Robinson

Illustrated by Melanie Sharp

Crabtree Publishing Company

www.crabtreebooks.com

Crabtree Publishing Company
www.crabtreebooks.com
1-800-387-7650

PMB 16A, 350 Fifth Ave.
Suite 3308,
New York, NY

616 Welland Ave.
St. Catharines, ON
L2M 5V6

Published by Crabtree Publishing in 2010

Series Editor: Jackie Hamley
Editors: Melanie Palmer, Reagan Miller
Series Advisor: Dr. Hilary Minns
Series Designer: Peter Scoulding
Editorial Director: Kathy Middleton

For Reece and Wilson – H.R.

First published in 2009
by Franklin Watts
(A division of Hachette Children's Books)

Library and Archives Canada Cataloguing in Publication

Robinson, Hilary, 1962-
Ted's party bus / Hilary Robinson ; illustrated by Melanie Sharp.

(Tadpoles)
ISBN 978-0-7787-3870-1 (bound).--
ISBN 978-0-7787-3901-2 (pbk.)

1. Readers (Primary). 2. Readers--Parties.
I. Sharp, Melanie II. Title. III. Series: Tadpoles (St. Catharines, Ont.)

PE1117.T33 2009c 428.6 C2009-903988-5

Library of Congress Cataloging-in-Publication Data

Robinson, Hilary, 1962-
Ted's party bus / by Hilary Robinson ; illustrated by Melanie Sharp.
p. cm. -- (Tadpoles)
Summary: Ted drives a bus around town picking up guests, but no one will tell him whose party it is.
ISBN 978-0-7787-3901-2 (pbk.) -- ISBN 978-0-7787-3870-1 (reinforced library binding)
[1. Parties--Fiction. 2. Bus drivers--Fiction. 3. Secrets--Fiction.] I. Sharp, Melanie, ill. II. Title. III. Series.

PZ7.R566175Ted 2010
[E]--dc22

2009025297

Ted drove the red party bus.

Ted stopped at Jack's house.

"Whose party is it?"
asked Ted.

“Wait and see,” said Jack’s mom.

Then Ted picked up Sam,

and Kate,

and Anna,

and Mohammed.

"Whose party are we going to?" asked Ted.

“You will find out soon,” the children said.

Ted picked up Ben,
Dan, and Jess.

"But whose party is it?" asked Ted.

"You will see,"
they all said.

“Please stop here,” said Jack’s mom.

"But that is my house!" said Ted.

“It is your party, Ted!”

65
today

Puzzle Time!

a

b

c

d

e

f

Put these pictures in the right order and retell the story!

curious

happy

puzzled

excited

Which words describe Ted and which describe the children?

Turn the page for the answers!

Notes for adults

TADPOLES are structured to provide support for early readers. The stories may also be used by adults for sharing with young children.

Starting to read alone can be daunting. **TADPOLES** help by providing visual support and repeating high frequency words and phrases. These books will both develop confidence and encourage reading and rereading for pleasure.

If you are reading this book with a child, here are a few suggestions:

1. Make reading fun! Choose a time to read when you and the child are relaxed and have time to share the story.
2. Talk about the story before you start reading. Look at the cover and the blurb. What might the story be about? Why might the child like it?
3. Encourage the child to reread the story, and to retell the story in their own words, using the illustrations to remind them what has happened.
4. Discuss the story and see if the child can relate it to their own experiences, or perhaps compare it to another story they know.
5. Give praise! Children learn best in a positive environment.

Answers

Here is the correct order:
1.e 2.a 3.f 4.d 5.c 6.b

Words to describe Ted: curious, puzzled
Words to describe the children: excited, happy

If you enjoyed this book, why not try another TADPOLES story?

At the End of the Garden
9780778738503 RLB
9780778738817 PB

Bad Luck, Lucy!
9780778738510 RLB
9780778738824 PB

Ben and the Big Balloon
9780778738602 RLB
9780778738916 PB

Crabby Gabby
9780778738527 RLB
9780778738831 PB

Dad's Cake
9780778738657 RLB
9780778738961 PB

Dad's Van
9780778738664 RLB
9780778738978 PB

The Dinosaur Next Door
9780778738732 RLB
9780778739043 PB

Five Teddy Bears
9780778738534 RLB
9780778738848 PB

I'm Taller Than You!
9780778738541 RLB
9780778738855 PB

Leo's New Pet
9780778738558 RLB
9780778738862 PB

Little Troll
9780778738565 RLB
9780778738879 PB

Mop Top
9780778738572 RLB
9780778738886 PB

My Auntie Susan
9780778738589 RLB
9780778738893 PB

My Big, New Bed
9780778738596 RLB
9780778738909 PB

Night, Night
9780778738671 RLB
9780778738985 PB

Over the Moon!
9780778738688 RLB
9780778738992 PB

Pirate Pete
9780778738619 RLB
9780778738923 PB

Rooster's Alarm
9780778738749 RLB
9780778739050 PB

Runny Honey
9780778738626 RLB
9780778738930 PB

The Sad Princess
9780778738725 RLB
9780778739036 PB

Sammy's Secret
9780778738633 RLB
9780778738947 PB

Sam's Sunflower
9780778738640 RLB
9780778738954 PB

Tag!
9780778738695 RLB
9780778739005 PB

Ted's Party Bus
9780778738701 RLB
9780778739012 PB

Tortoise Races Home
9780778738718 RLB
9780778739029 PB

Printed in the USA—CG